Hazel Z. Lindee

Linda L. Barton

Cheryl
I love
you dear friend
Enjoy

Linda L. Barton

Dedicated to the Hazel Z. in us all....

Hazel Z. Lindee is ever so good!

She follows the path like she should,

silent and strong like a redwood.

But her mind fills

like a huge black anthill,

with ideas that crawl and spill…
They just won't sit still.

Hazel Z. Lindee can settle

like her Auntie's green teakettle.

This is quite monumental,

because her mind is like

fresh sweet peas

with singing, summer chickadees,

and old secret skeleton keys.

Hazel Z. Lindee is well mannered,

and that, to some, seems to matter.

But her mind is a splatter

of upside down platters

-- pizza pies and rice pilaf.

Her thoughts

(-- if known --)

might make people scoff.

That's why, at times, she looks so far off...

Hazel Z. Lindee eats all her food

(at least, tries every food).

Her thoughts are like

pots of minestrone soup, stewing.

You'd think she'd learn,

but ideas seem to burn

like rye toast left too long.

But her mind does return!

Hazel Z. Lindee can read a library book.

But it is tricky

as her mind leaves its nook

and meanders like a brook

finding grasshoppers in jars

and long-nosed fish called gars,

even a few falling stars.

Hazel Z. Lindee can dress

without a fit or mess.

But her insides are bold

and she will unfold

like green, rumpled, rivers of ribbons --

brown buttons in the shape of gibbons,

beyond her bandanas that are crimson.

13

Hazel Z. Lindee can keep clean

like a fancy washing machine.

But her mind keeps sloshing --

messy with whirls,

then two naughty squirrels,

and a thousand and one oyster's pearls.

Hazel Z. Lindee is not

teacher's pet.

Her brain is set

to think, plan and get

tree houses for blue jays,

dragons that stray,

pumpkins in the fresh cut hay.

And Saturday,

who can play?

Hazel Z. Lindee is sweet

like dandelions in bare feet.

But her mind might just cheat,

taking her far far away

from her chores for the day.

She has ideas at play --

or how to fix or change everything

like kites, daffodils and a swing.

Even a bell that won't ring!

Hazel Z. Lindee is special

like a wisdom tooth!

She rarely makes a goof,

always telling the truth.

But in her head she is tricky,

full of pranks and sticky…

and at times even a bit icky.

Hazel Z. Lindee goes to bed on time.

But her head stays awake to rhyme

(snails, pails and tails…)

Then her dreams,

slow to invade,

may fade

or make a wild parade.

She wonders,

should she be afraid?

Of how fast it all goes by…

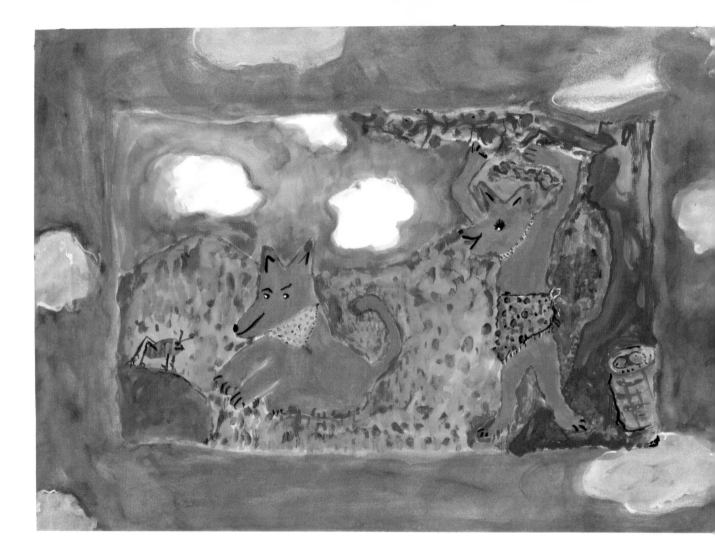

Hazel Z. Lindee can, for a while focus.

But to her, focus takes a bit of hocus-pocus!

She wonders,

her mind on the move...

Auntie says, "Ah, it will improve.

Your mind is the sky,

and the clouds are your thoughts.

They come in every way,

Float and glide every way.

Move - that's what thoughts and clouds do".

Hazel Z. Lindee said,
"I am okay with that.
For the whole day,
I will stay here,
Watching clouds and thoughts
billow to and fro."

She did exactly that.
Because, she is
Hazel Z. Lindee
and could.

Linda L. Barton splits her time between Lopez Island, Washington and Santa Cruz, California. She has worked , sometimes passionately, as a child therapist, potter, poet, gardener, and traveler. Currently, she is writing the children's books she wished she had when she was growing up. To contact her, please visit her website: LindaLBarton.com.

Thanks to everyone who helped. You know who you are. And please know you will get you very own sign copy from Hazel herself.

ed

"_____ oops"!